Sky and the Magical Steelband

Anthony Francis and Hannah James

odbbookz

READING THE SUN OUT

Sky and the Magical Steelband
Authored by Anthony Francis, Illustrated by Hannah James

Copywrite Anthony Francis 2021 Published by ODBBKZLTD, Enfield, United Kingdom

All rights reserved 2022 Anthony Francis The Author asserts the moral right to be identified as the Author of this work. This book is sold subject to the conditions it is not, by trade or otherwise circulated in any form of binding or cover other than that in which it is published. No part of this publication may be reproduced, stored in a retrieval system or transmitted in any form or by any means (electronic, mechanical, photocopying, recording or otherwise) without prior written permission from the Author or Publisher.

ISBN: 979-8-88940-575-7

First Edition March 2022
Second Edition March 2024

Dedications

This book is dedicated first to my father 'Augustine Pepe Francis' MBE', then to my youngest daughter, Sky Amenti Francis, whose joy and passion for life and playing the Steel pans, can be an inspiration to us all. It is also dedicated to all of my other wonderful, talented Children; 'Tafari, Solomon, Daniel, Zion, Osiris, Isis, and Nephthys', who have all learned to play the steelpans at some point in their lives, but most of all these books are dedicated to my Grandchildren and all the Children of the world,(the future) whom I hope will have hours of fun and enjoyment from reading these books and learning about the Steelband, the Carnival, the music, the history and the culture of Trinidad and Tobago, and most of all learning how to play the Steelpans.

It is also dedicated to all of the players from the Ebony Steelband, both past and present, and to all the Steelpan players and Teachers from around the world, in that, they may be able to share with their young children, just some of the excitement, passion, and joy that we have had from playing these instruments, listening to them, teaching them to people from all around the world, and learning about the art of making the steelpans and the story of how the steel bands began.

This is the FLAG of
Trinidad and Tobago,
This is the country where
the Steel Bands were born.

Last year Sky Amenti had the most amazing day at school! She got the 'Biggest Surprise' that she thought was so cool.

It was a visit from her dad and the Ebony Steelband and now everyone in the school was a big Steelband fan.

As she wondered to herself how the Steelband had begun, her dad then told the story to everyone.
That day, the whole school learned some exciting things, how the Steelbands began from some small metal bins.

That day, when Sky got home, she said, "Please tell me again!"
When her dad saw her excitement, he just could not refrain.
"Okay, come over here and have a seat next to me,
And I'll tell you again how the Steelbands came to be."

It was a long time ago, back in Trinidad and Tobago,
When the parents of the village, to the Carnival,
they would go.
All the children were left with their grandparents for the day,
and after eating their porridge, they would all go and play.

One child called 'Ellie Mannette' who loved to play cricket gathered all his friends, but they could not find a wicket. So, they decided to use Uncle Winston Spree's bin, which got dented so much, that the top was sunken in.

When Uncle Winston got home and he saw all the dents,
He was so disappointed that he needed to vent.
So, with a stick and a stone he banged the dents out.
Then suddenly, suddenly, he gave a loud shout.

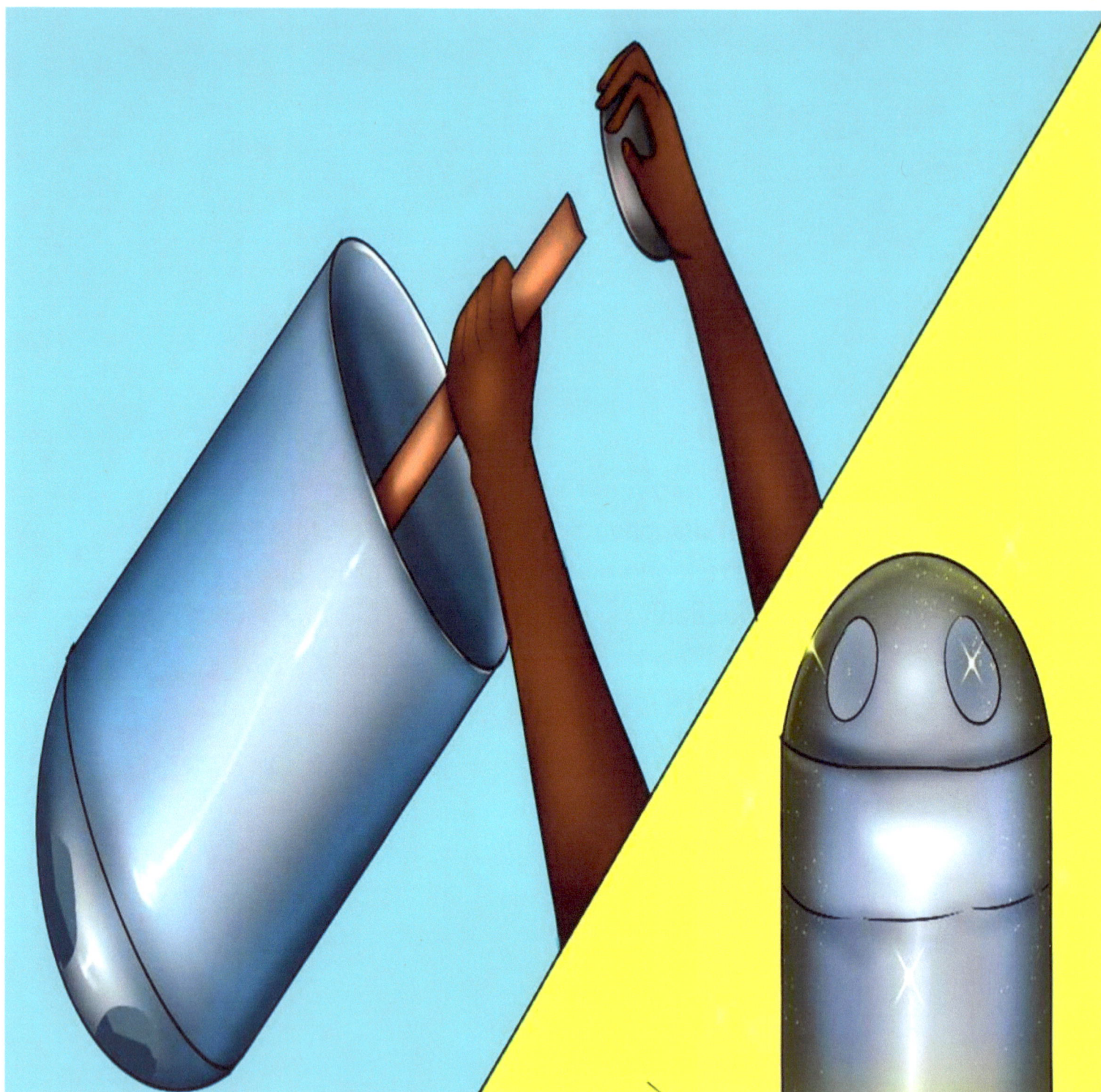

"Musical notes are coming from my old metal bin!"
So, he kept hitting and hitting and did not give in.
Until he got four different notes—this was the first of its kind and 'Mary had a little lamb', was the first song he could find.

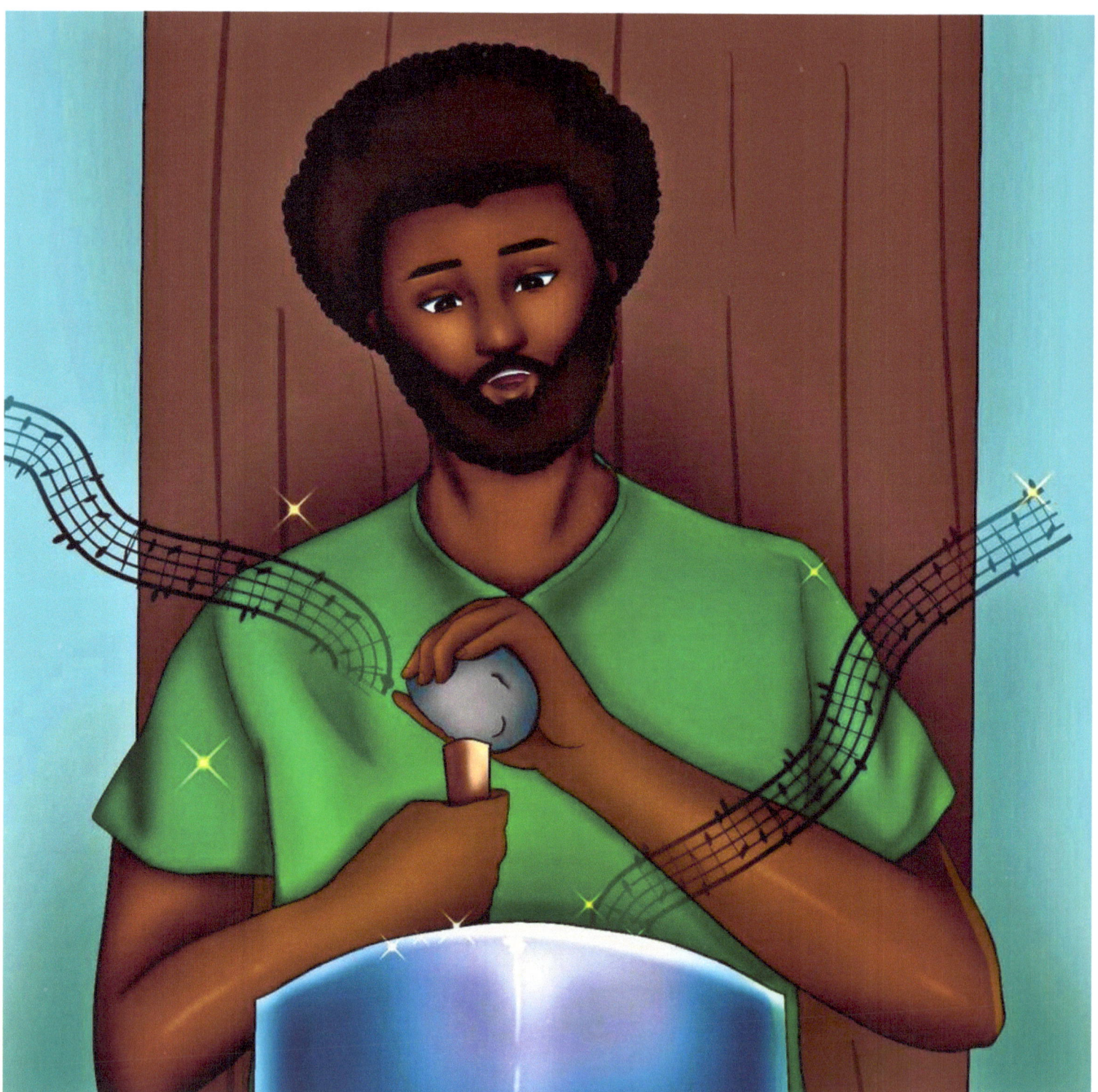

The Four-Note 'Ping Pong' was the new drum in town,
The first 'Steel Pan' did make such a beautiful sound.
And he was so excited about his brand-new discovery,
he showed his new steelpan off to everybody.

And when he explained just what he had done,
All the men in the village said they could make one.
They added more and more notes, 5-6-7 and then 8,

Then a man called Neville Jules came bursting in through the gate and he shouted to everyone, "Wait, wait, wait."

"I've found another new sound, and it's called the "Du Dup Bass!'

Next year 'PING PONG' and 'Du Dup' will shake down the place."

At the Carnival the following year, the new Steelband appeared,
And Winston and Neville were crowned "Men of the Year."

"The end," Daddy said, "and it's soon time for bed,
but there is one more thing that I still haven't read."
He gave Sky a big book, and she opened it to see,
there were pictures of how the Steelbands used to be.
Sky was so happy, she shouted, "Yippee!"
Then she turned every page with excitement and glee.

She now knew herself and felt confident to say,
She would follow in Dad's footsteps and learn how to play.
She took up her dad's sticks, and she practised each day,
And knew that she, too, would invent,
something brand new one
day.

So, for the whole of that day, from beginning to the end, 'The Steelband' had become Sky's brand-new best-friend.

THE END

So What have we learned today?

Question 1: What country did the steel bands come from?

T-------- and T-----

Question 2: Who invented 'Ping Pong'?

W------- S----- S-----

Question 3: Who invented 'Du Dup'?

N------- J------

Question 4: What celebration did the Parents attend when the children stayed with their Grand parents?

The C--------

Question 4: This is the flag of what country? T-------- and T-----

Check out part 1 'Sky's Big Steelband Surprise' and find out how Sky learned about the Steelbands.

About the Author

Anthony "Dpan" Francis first began learning to play the steel pan instrument at the young age of nine. After attending the 'Notting Hill Carnival with his mother at age five, where he first saw and heard his father's band the Ebony Steelband play, from that day onwards he was totally captivated and mesmerized by the beautiful sound of the instrument and the culture of "Trinidad and Tobago."

So began his lifelong journey of playing, teaching, arranging and producing music with the only instrument to be invented in the 20th century: the Steel Pan.

This is his first book in the series of 'Sky's Steelband Adventures' and one of many to be written about his love for the Steelband.

About the Illustrator

Hannah James is 19 years old, Born in Trinidad and Tobago, from the village of Arima, she has always loved art and had a dream to become a digital artist one day, she is now studying animation at the University of Trinidad and Tobago, She loves to draw characters and colorful artwork.

I discovered ShyShy Arts services on Fiverr.com and we are now working on our third book together.

"Check out
'Sky's Big Steelband Surprise',
and Look out for more Book titles
and merchandise from
ODBBOOKZ
and
'Sky's Steelband Adventures'
www.odbbookz.com
and visit
the Ebony Steelband Trust
www.ebony-steelband-trust.co.uk

And dont forget to connect with us on

odbbookz

READING THE SUN OUT

www.ingramcontent.com/pod-product-compliance
Lightning Source LLC
Chambersburg PA
CBHW041923030225
21332CB00034B/318